UH-OH,
ROLLO!

NOTE FROM THE AUTHOR:

"Uh-oh, Rollo!" is a phrase that my partner,
Anna Dewdney, used to say around the house
when the real Rollo was up to his usual mischief.
The inspiration for this book is from her.

ABOUT THE AUTHOR:

Reed Duncan is an author as well as a former
reading instructor, teacher, and school administrator.
He lives in Vermont. The Rollo stories are based on
Reed and his real-life, rambunctious bulldog.

PENGUIN WORKSHOP
An Imprint of Penguin Random House LLC, New York

Text copyright © 2019 by Reed Duncan. Illustrations copyright © 2019 by Penguin Random House LLC.
All rights reserved. First published in hardcover in 2019 by Penguin Workshop. This paperback edition
published in 2020 by Penguin Workshop, an imprint of Penguin Random House LLC, New York.
PENGUIN and PENGUIN WORKSHOP are trademarks of Penguin Books Ltd, and
the W colophon is a registered trademark of Penguin Random House LLC.
Manufactured in China.

Visit us online at www.penguinrandomhouse.com.

Library of Congress Control Number: 2019945283

ISBN 9781524792442   10 9 8 7 6 5 4 3 2 1

UH-OH, ROLLO!

by REED DUNCAN
illustrated by KEITH FRAWLEY

PENGUIN WORKSHOP

Rollo is a good dog.

He loves to play.

But sometimes he does things that get him into trouble.

Rollo loves to dig,
but sometimes he digs too much.

He does not wipe his paws
before he comes back inside.

ROLL-O . . .

Rollo loves to chew,
but sometimes he chews
things he should not.

Rollo loves to climb,
but sometimes he climbs
where he should not.

UH-OH, ROLLO!

SiLLY ROLL-O . . .

Rollo likes to chase things.

But sometimes he chases
things he should not.

UH-OH, ROLLO!

WHAM!

ROLL-O . . .

Rollo loves to eat.

But sometimes he eats
things he should not.

BLECK!

Rollo feels sick.
Poor Rollo.

But there's one thing that Rollo
loves to do the most.

And that's to say he's sorry.